ROTHERHAM LIBRARY & INFORMATION SERVICE

This book must be returned by the date specified at the time of issue as
the DATE DUE FOR RETURN.
The loan may be extended (personally, by post, telephone or online) for
a further period if the book is not required by another reader, by quoting
the above number / author / title.

Enquiries: 01709 336774

www.rotherham.gov.uk/libraries

For Ava and Scarlett

First published 2011 by Macmillan Children's Books
This edition published 2014 by Macmillan Children's Books
a division of Macmillan Publishers Limited
20 New Wharf Road, London N1 9RR
Basingstoke and Oxford
Associated companies throughout the world
www.panmacmillan.com

ISBN: 978-1-4472-3695-5

Text and illustrations copyright © Julie Monks 2011
Moral rights asserted

2 4 6 8 9 7 5 3 1

A CIP catalogue record for this book is available from the British Library.

Printed in China

MARCELLO MOUSE
and the MASKED BALL

Julie Monks

MACMILLAN CHILDREN'S BOOKS

Marcello Mouse lived alone in a dark hole,
along a dark canal, in the darkest corner of Venice.
But he longed for warmth, and he longed for music,
and he longed for light.

The winter had been long, the coldest Venice had
ever known. But with a twitch of his tiny nose,
Marcello could tell that spring was on its way,
and with spring came a magical event!

Marcello had spent the cold months preparing;
stitching and sewing, waiting and wondering.
At last, the special day arrived. In the distance,
Marcello Mouse heard a beautiful song . . .

"One by one they come,
on the most magical night of all.
With a rustle of silk and a jingle of bells,
off to the magical ball."

With a squeak and a leap and a flick of his tail, Marcello slipped out of his door. He hopped up the steps over the bridge . . .

. . . and along the canal, singing to himself as he scampered towards the twinkling lights in the distance.

With each mouse step the lights grew brighter and the music grew louder.

Marcello drew close to the Grand Palace . . .

. . . home of the Magical Masked Ball.

Marcello skipped lightly up the steps, smoothed down his fur, and paused. For this little mouse was not invited to the ball. But as he stood in the doorway, his fur felt warm and the air smelled sweet.

Quick as a flash he slipped inside!
How DARING! How BOLD!

Marcello Mouse in a room full of CATS!

But Marcello was prepared.

He had made a cunning disguise!
They'll never guess, thought
Marcello with a grin.

And with a leap of joy he followed his nose
to a table full of food.

He tasted fine wine and wonderful cheese, and
nibbled at cakes that were sugary sweet.

He was lively and funny and charming.
"*What a nice fellow,*" the cats all agreed.

Then came the call, "*Let the dancing begin.*"
Light as a feather, Marcello leaped to the floor . . .

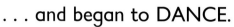 . . . and began to DANCE.

He twisted and turned,

he skipped and he swung,

he tripped and he twizzled,

then suddenly . . . STOPPED!

Not a whisker twitched and not a paw moved.

"That's no cat, it's a MOUSE!"
Poor Marcello's tail began to quiver in fright.

Then he let out a terrified "squeak."

"I'll be Mice Cream by midnight!"
cried Marcello, dashing for
the door. Swerving and
skidding, he shot across
the floor.

He sped along the hallway and scampered down
the steps.

He darted along the canal and tumbled over
the bridge.

He ran without stopping and without looking back,
until the bright lights of the ball were far behind him.

Back in his dark little
mouse hole, Marcello
shivered and trembled
in fright.

"One by one they ran,
on the most magical night of all,
With a rustle of silk and a jingle of bells,
away from the pussycat ball."

"I've been so silly,"
he sobbed.
"They could have
eaten me up!"
Slowly and sadly
Marcello put his
outfit away.

Then he curled up into a little ball and tried his hardest to fall asleep.

All of a sudden, there came a loud knock!
"CATS!"

Trembling, Marcello peered around the door.
But there on the mat, instead of a cat, was a
large, golden envelope. And written on the
envelope was the name, *Marcello Mouse*.

"For me?" he squeaked. "I've never had a letter."

The cats of Venice cordially invite brave Marcello Mouse, the amazing dancing mouse, to be guest of honour at the Summer Ball.

Marcello hopped and leaped for joy. "They weren't going to eat me, they liked me!" Marcello Mouse was a happy mouse once more.

And so, when the evening arrived, a small, smartly dressed mouse left his dark hole, along a dark canal, in the darkest corner of Venice, and made his way to the grandest ball.

And there upon a sparkling stage, Marcello Mouse,
the amazing dancing mouse, received the warmest
welcome of all.

The End